C000157130

Vengeanc

by Yukiko Motoya

Translation by Kyoko Yoshida
and Andy Bragen

A SAMUEL FRENCH ACTING EDITION

FOUNDED 1830

SAMUELFRENCH.COM

ISBN 978-0-573-70018-7   Printed in U.S.A.   #28087

(*NANASE exits into the back room.* **HIDENORI**, *tired, lies down on the bed, then, after a moment…*)

HIDENORI. Nanase, I'm going for a jog.

NANASE. *(from offstage)* But what about dinner?

HIDENORI. I'll eat when I get back.

NANASE. *(from offstage)* Okay. Have a good jog.

(**HIDENORI**, *casting an eye toward the back room, skillfully removes a panel from the ceiling. He slides himself up into the attic and peeks in through the three inch space between the panels. After a little while, he sees* **NANASE** *return to the room. She opens a notebook and starts writing something down. She gets restless, then, as if she just remembered something, rises to go to the bathroom.*)

NANASE. If I come up with a joke I'll let myself go to the bathroom. *(She sits down again.)* If I want to urinate, I must come up with a good joke.

(*The doorbell rings.* **NANASE** *starts to panic. The doorbell keeps ringing.* **NANASE** *moves toward the door. She's trembling, on the verge of crying.*)

BANJO. *(from outside)* Hello!

NANASE. *(anxiously looking up)…*

BANJO. Excuse me! This is Mr. Yamane's place, isn't it?

NANASE. *(moving toward the door)* Who is it?

BANJO. Hi. I'm Banjo, a colleague of Mr. Yamane's at work.

NANASE. You're not here selling magazine subscriptions, are you?

BANJO. No. I'm his colleague, Banjo.

NANASE. Colleague Ban-jo.

BANJO. That's a funny way to say it, but anyway…. I came here to have a chat with Mr. Yamane, 'cause, how should I put this, it's something that I don't feel quite comfortable addressing at work, so /

(**NANASE** *slowly and carefully opens the door.*)

Well …so… *(looking* **NANASE** *up and down)* Are you his girlfriend?

NANASE. …He's not in right now.

BANJO. What?

NANASE. Daddy's out on an errand.

BANJO. Oh, okay. …Do you know where he went and when he'll be back?

(**NANASE** *falls silent, then, trembling, she bows deeply.*)

NANASE. I'm so sorry!

BANJO. What? Why are you apologizing? So he's not home – no big deal. Well then, what about his cell phone? Give me his number, and I'll /

NANASE. *(interrupting)* I don't know it! *(crying)* I'm sorry!

BANJO. Hey, no need to apologize! I'm confused. I mean, maybe I'm the one who should be apologizing. I'm sorry!

NANASE. *(mortified, sinking in shame)* AGGHHHHH!

BANJO. *(taken aback)* Ohhhhhh!

NANASE. …

BANJO. What's the matter?

NANASE. I'll give you money.

BANJO. What? Why?

NANASE. *(retrieving her wallet from a drawer)* Because I made you apologize even though this is the first time we've met. I definitely made you frustrated, didn't I? So, before it's too late, here's two thousand /

BANJO. But no. I'm not frustrated. If you give me money, I won't know what to do with it.

(*pause*)

NANASE. So, you really didn't get…

BANJO. I didn't get frustrated.

NANASE. Really?

(**BANJO** *nods.*)

NANASE. *(breathing a sigh of relief)* That was close.

(**BANJO** *watches* **NANASE**'s *response with suspicion.*)

BANJO. Okay…I guess I'll wait somewhere nearby. When Yamane comes home, can you ask him to call my /

NANASE. *(interrupting)* Wait.

BANJO. Yes?

NANASE. *(anxiously)* Would you like to wait inside?

BANJO. You mean, it's okay?

NANASE. Because if I make you wait outside, you'll get…

BANJO. I won't get frustrated. But if it's okay to wait inside…

NANASE. Please.

BANJO. Thank you.

NANASE. Oh!

BANJO. *(surprised)* What is it?

NANASE. Before you come in…

> (**NANASE** *pulls the top of her sweatshirt over her head, forming a monkish hood.*)

…please come in.

BANJO. Thank you.

> (**BANJO** *enters the room cautiously and sits on the cushion which* **NANASE** *has brought out for him. Some moments of silence, then…*)

BANJO. May I ask what…

NANASE. Is it bothering you?

BANJO. I wouldn't say bothering…but I'm not sure what exactly…

NANASE. You see, I'm doing this because we're alone here, but I let you come inside. So, you might start thinking something like, "What's up with this girl? Is she hitting on me or what?" Right?

BANJO. That's hard to answer.

NANASE. And then, even though I'm the one who led you to think that way, I might say something like, "I didn't intend anything of the sort!" and then you'd be mortified with shame. I shouldn't do that to you, should I? So it's up to me to take responsibility for the moment where you might be misled /

BANJO. What? So are you saying that if we do it, you'll take responsibility?

NANASE. My point is…to avoid leading you on, I'm doing this…

(*She gestures toward the changes she's made to her appearance.*)

BANJO. Okay…I see…

(**NANASE** *pulls her sweatpants high above her waist.*)

NANASE. Is it not enough?

BANJO. No, it's plenty.

NANASE. Whew. That was close.

BANJO. Uh-huh.

(**BANJO** *agrees, although he's not sure what he is agreeing to. An awkward pause.* **NANASE** *keeps glancing toward the bathroom.*)

BANJO. So, you're Yamane's little girl?

NANASE. I'm his roommate.

BANJO. You mean, partner?

NANASE. No.

BANJO. (*looking around the room*) This doesn't seem like a roommate situation.

NANASE. No.

BANJO. What are you then, if I may ask?

NANASE. We're strangers, living together.

BANJO. But you called him "Daddy" earlier.

NANASE. I call him "Daddy," but we're not related.

BANJO. How old is "Daddy" anyway?

NANASE. He'll be thirty next week.

BANJO. …

NANASE. Is something wrong?

BANJO. Oh no, nothing. I mean, so, you guys aren't lovers, and you're not family, but still, here you are living together. You must get along with each other really well, then.

NANASE. We don't…

BANJO. …get along well either… what's your name?

NANASE. Ogawa.

BANJO. First name?

NANASE. Nanase.

BANJO. How old are you, Nanase?

NANASE. I'm 26.

BANJO. What do you do all day?

NANASE. Um, well, all day I work on jokes and…

BANJO. Jokes?

NANASE. Nothing.

BANJO. All right.

    (**BANJO** *stands up and starts looking over the room.*)

BANJO. Wow. A bunk bed! Yamane sleeps here?

NANASE. Daddy sleeps on the top bunk and I sleep on the bottom.

BANJO. *(as if talking to a child)* But of course. Fathers and daughters never share beds.

NANASE. I guess not.

BANJO. Wow, this bed is narrow.

    (**BANJO** *lies down on the top bunk.* **NANASE** *keeps glancing hesitantly toward the bathroom.*)

NANASE. I have to go to the…

BANJO. You know, that whole thing about frustrating someone…

NANASE. …Yes?

BANJO. Are you always so worried about stuff like that?

NANASE. I'm always imagining other people's feelings.

BANJO. Imagining their feelings? Like how?

NANASE. Like…if I'm talking with someone, and say, I have to go to the bathroom.

BANJO. Uh huh.

NANASE. If I cut off the conversation, it's a turn off, so I try to hold it in, right?

BANJO. Well, if it was a really engaging conversation…

NANASE. But if I wait for the right moment, even if that moment comes and I say it, then that person will know that I'd been thinking about going the whole time, right? That I was hoping for the conversation to end soon, or that I was thinking like, just spit it out you sloth, or something like that. When I imagine being seen that way by others, I just can't…

BANJO. Most people don't think that much.

NANASE. That's how I am.

BANJO. I see. So…*(staring at* **NANASE** *closely)*…may I go to the bathroom?

NANASE. Oh, sure!

*(***BANJO*** goes to the bathroom. ***NANASE*** paces restlessly. She's holding it in. Eventually, ***BANJO*** returns from the bathroom.)*

NANASE. Okay, so it's my…

BANJO. *(blocking* **NANASE***'s path)* My apologies if I'm mistaken, but…

NANASE. …mistaken?

BANJO. You are a good looking girl.

NANASE. …

BANJO. Why are you dressed in such…dumpy sweats?

NANASE. Well, because…I was born in these clothes!

BANJO. Are you near-sighted?

NANASE. Yes, I am.

BANJO. Hmmm.

NANASE. But I…

BANJO. Yes?

NANASE. Nothing.

BANJO. Okay.

*(***NANASE*** can barely stand holding it in. She is breathing louder and louder. Finally, she squats down.)*

BANJO. Are you all right?

NANASE. With what?

BANJO. Well, I don't know with what, but…

NANASE. Never mind. I'm just…remembering something funny, and…it makes me laugh.

(She laughs.)

BANJO. Is that it? Really, are you all right?

NANASE. I'm all right, I'm all right.

(She laughs.)

BANJO. If you really are, that's good but…I think I should get…

NANASE. What?

BANJO. I should get going, 'cause it doesn't seem like Yamane is coming back anytime soon.

NANASE. …okay…

BANJO. Would you tell him that Banjo stopped….

NANASE. *(interrupting)* Yes! I'll tell him!

BANJO. Thanks. So long, Nanase.

*(**BANJO** exits. **NANASE** sees him off while squatting. Eventually, she stands up. She has wet her pants.)*

NANASE. It's much better than frustrating people!

HIDENORI. …

*(**NANASE** goes to the bathroom. **HIDENORI** watches her intensely from the attic. Strong spotlight on **HIDENORI**, then, slowly, lights fade.)*

-5-

(**HIDENORI** *is sitting in the room with the switches.*
BANJO *comes running into the room.*)

BANJO. Sorry. I was having lunch, and...

HIDENORI. ...

BANJO. By the way, Takamura and the guys are talking
about grabbing drinks after work today. Would you
like to join us?

HIDENORI. If I'm in the mood.

BANJO. You always say that, but you never show up. What
keeps you so busy at home?

HIDENORI. I jog.

BANJO. Jog?

HIDENORI. I run along the embankment.

BANJO. Really? That's a surprise.

HIDENORI. Is it?

BANJO. Yeah, because, Mr. Yamane, you don't strike me as
the athletic type.

HIDENORI. Most marathon runners look just like me.

BANJO. That's true. I shouldn't make assumptions. Sorry
about that.

HIDENORI. I don't mind.

(**HIDENORI** *is sitting still on the chair.* **BANJO** *starts
smoking next to him. He looks completely different from
the last time - very relaxed.*)

BANJO. So...I have a little proposal for you.

HIDENORI. A proposal?

BANJO. Your roommate, Nanase. Does she fancy herself a
comedian or something?

HIDENORI. ...

(**HIDENORI** *looks at* **BANJO.**)

BANJO. I was thinking, that could be the case. She said that she was working on some jokes, and that notebook… I happened to see it 'cause it was lying open on the desk. Apparently, she's studying comedy. Is she developing a solo act or, could it be… *(pointing his finger at* **HIDENORI***)* …a duo?

HIDENORI. She's doing it on her own.

BANJO. Right. Of course. What I meant to say is that she might need a partner.

(The music could start around here.)

I know a girl, she's my girlfriend actually, who would make a perfect partner for Nanase. She's a seriously funny girl. Nanase is…pretty, but she doesn't seem to have much of a gift for comedy. Azusa would be perfect for it. She works for a corporation, but that's totally not where she belongs. She'd fit in much better at a comedy club.

HIDENORI. …

BANJO. And so, to give Azusa her chance too, I want to introduce her to Nanase.

(The music ends. **HIDENORI** *is flipping the two switches simultaneously.)*

I truly appreciate you doing this.

HIDENORI. You didn't have to come all the way to my house to ask me that.

BANJO. But I couldn't ask you at work, you know.

HIDENORI. About your proposal…

BANJO. Yes.

HIDENORI. I have to decline. That girl is incapable of communicating.

*(***HIDENORI** *starts to exit.)*

BANJO. Okay…but you know what?

HIDENORI. What?

BANJO. It may already be too late.

HIDENORI. …

-6-

(AZUSA, gloomy, stands in the middle of the room, smoking. She is wearing an expensive designer dress. NANASE, tense, is seated on the floor.)

AZUSA. Ashtray!

NANASE. Yes, of course!

(NANASE puts out an ashtray for AZUSA.)

AZUSA. I can't believe it's you.

NANASE. It's a big coincidence...

AZUSA. Why are you living in a place like this? Are you poor?

NANASE. Yes. I guess I am a little poor.

AZUSA. You're not working?

NANASE. I'm not working.

AZUSA. Why?

NANASE. Daddy tells me to stay home, so...

AZUSA. He tells you to stay home and make up jokes?

NANASE. Yes.

AZUSA. And he tells you to make him laugh?

NANASE. It's not like an order. It's just that his job seems to take a big toll on him, so...

AZUSA. Yeah, I heard. Banjo and Yamane are a team at work, right? They say that you can't know which is the dummy switch, but that's nonsense. Banjo was furious the other day, saying that the odds are too high.

NANASE. Oh yeah?

AZUSA. He says that it's driving him crazy.

NANASE. Tell me about it! I've never managed to make Daddy laugh, not even once.

AZUSA. *(looking at the notebook)* How long have you been doing this?

NANASE. Since I was 24, so...

AZUSA. *(surprised)* It's been two years?

NANASE. But really, I'm doing it 'cause I want to. It's much better than sitting around and just waiting for the revenge.

AZUSA. The revenge?

NANASE. Uh-huh. I've been waiting for it, for all this time. Azusa, do you want something to drink?

AZUSA. No, I don't. What did you just say? That you're waiting for what?

NANASE. For the revenge. Daddy has to take revenge on me. I did something to deserve it.

(pause)

AZUSA. All right. It doesn't make much sense, but for the sake of conversation, I get that he doesn't like you. But why are you just waiting? Don't you want to get it over with? You're not going to be killed or anything, are you?

NANASE. He said that it'll be something so awful that I'd rather be killed, that his revenge will be the worst in the history of humankind.

(pause)

AZUSA. What kind of revenge will it be?

NANASE. Well, that's what Daddy's been working on. It's hard to come up with such a radical idea. *(shyly)* Besides, he has extremely high standards, Mr. Perfection, you know…

AZUSA. How long have you been waiting?

NANASE. Six years, though of course it's been twelve since the big day.

AZUSA. …

NANASE. Azusa?

AZUSA. Wait, I don't understand. Twelve years?

NANASE. That's right.

AZUSA. So you've been resented by him for twelve years?

NANASE. It's a little more complicated than that, but for six years, at least.

AZUSA. For six years, you've been waiting here for that guy's vengeance?

NANASE. …yes.

AZUSA. Are you stupid or something?

NANASE. I'm not sure…

(pause)

AZUSA. I'm going home.

NANASE. What? Why so soon? Come on, Azusa. Won't you be my standup partner? Or did I do something to upset you? Oh, could it be the hair? That nose hair sticking out from your nostril that I noticed while we were talking but didn't mention? Are you upset because that was the only thing I was thinking about during our whole conversation?

AZUSA. It's a fashion statement!

NANASE. Oh, okay. I'm sorry I didn't…

*(**AZUSA** strides toward the door. **NANASE** starts to follow.)*

NANASE. Azusa.

AZUSA. Let me tell you something. I too, haven't forgotten. I still remember what you did to me in high school.

*(**AZUSA** glares at **NANASE** and exits.)*

-7-

(**BANJO**, *alone, enters. He takes a ringing cell phone out of his pocket.*)

BANJO. Hello? Hey, Azusa. How'd it go?...A classmate? You guys went all through school together? Wow, that's an amazing coincidence! Then again, this is your hometown. *(calling offstage)* Yes, I'll be there in a moment. *(back to the cell phone)* But that's perfect for our plan, because if you guys already know each other, she won't be suspicious about...Huh? You don't like her? Don't be jealous - though I guess I understand how you feel. I just thought that she was a strange girl and got curious... *(calling offstage)* Yes. Yes, I'm sorry! *(on the cell phone)* Hey, easy does it! All I want you to do is to find out more about them. ...Are you serious? Ha, ha! I knew there was something between them! ...Twelve years! That's amazing. Hey, Azusa, visit them often. Become good friends, all right? But of course, this is just the beginning. When it comes to those two, I have the feeling that we still don't know the half of it.

(**BANJO** *hangs up the phone and exits.*)

-8-

(Music. **HIDENORI***, in his pajamas, is using the hair dryer.* **NANASE** *is also present. On the table, a plate of sliced apples.)*

HIDENORI. *(turning off the hair dryer)* I don't want apples.

NANASE. …okay.

(She starts to eat the apples.)

HIDENORI. I don't want them.

NANASE. …Yes.

*(***NANASE** *nods and takes the plate to the back room. She returns, coughing.)*

HIDENORI. Did you catch a cold?

NANASE. Yes, but I'm not feverish.

HIDENORI. Taking any medicine?

NANASE. We just ran out, but, really, I'm really all right.

HIDENORI. I don't want to catch it, okay?

NANASE. I see.

HIDENORI. How'd it go today?

NANASE. I practiced a gag.

HIDENORI. Gags are golden.

NANASE. But I just can't seem to get it right.

HIDENORI. Try it out.

NANASE. Okay… *(timidly, flapping her arms)* Well, I just flew in from Osaka, and boy, are my planes, I mean arms, tired.

*(***NANASE** *coughs.)*

HIDENORI. Are you all right?

NANASE. Yes, I'm fine. What did you think of the gag?

HIDENORI. It's no good.

NANASE. Why not? It's an old favorite!

HIDENORI. That gag won't work for you. Find something else.

NANASE. But why…?

HIDENORI. The harder you try, the more absurd it gets.

NANASE. *(crying)* But why? I've been practicing so hard... ! My arms, my arms, my arms...

(throwing herself at **HIDENORI***)*

Please, help me!

*(***HIDENORI*** looks down at* **NANASE** *who squats down and coughs violently.)*

HIDENORI. I've got a better one for you, Nanase. It's called "the Comăneci."

NANASE. "Comăneci, the gymnast?"

HIDENORI. Watch me. I'll show you. With practice, you'll master this one.

NANASE. Okay.

HIDENORI. Comăneci...Comăneci...Comăneci... Comăneci...*

*(***HIDENORI*** keeps doing the Comăneci mechanically.* **NANASE** *watches him intensely.)*

NANASE. *(covering her face with her hands)* I'm scared!

HIDENORI. Of what?

NANASE. Nothing. Never mind.

*(***NANASE*** has a coughing fit.)*

HIDENORI. Let's just call it a day.

NANASE. But I ...

HIDENORI. Never mind. That's it for today.

NANASE. All right, then...Oh, I forgot to tell you, a woman came by to visit today. She said that your colleague sent her.

HIDENORI. To do what?

NANASE. She said that she'd help me with a new comedy routine to make you laugh. I think it's a good idea. I'm talentless, and Azusa's funny looking, so if we work hard together, maybe we'll make a good team.

---

*The joke refers to Nadia Comăneci's high bikini line. Hidenori mechanically moves his arms diagonally from his crotch to his waist, indicating the cut of her bikini.

HIDENORI. You're going to work with her?

NANASE. Don't worry. I'll be careful not to irritate her.

HIDENORI. …

NANASE. By the way, you jogged for a long time today. How far did you go?

HIDENORI. All the way to Jusco.

NANASE. That far? Is your knee all right?

(**HIDENORI** *climbs up to the upper bunk of the bed, limping.*)

NANASE. Are you sure you don't want to switch beds?

HIDENORI. Are you saying that you want to be on top?

(*pause*)

(**NANASE** *turns on the bedside lamp and turns off the room light. She crawls into bed.*)

NANASE. Do you think that you'll come up with it tomorrow?

HIDENORI. I will come up with it tomorrow.

(**NANASE** *crosses off another day on the calendar.*)

NANASE. Good night, Daddy.

(**NANASE** *turns off the lamp.*)

(*blackout*)

-9-

*(**HIDENORI** and **NANASE**'s room. **AZUSA** is holding **NANASE** by the hair and yelling at her. **HIDENORI** is watching in silence.)*

AZUSA. You just don't get it, do you? This is supposed to be a skit! Why am I playing a wounded monkey and staggering around the room alone? Huh?

NANASE. There's no particular reason. I thought it might be avant garde.

AZUSA. Way too avant garde! Besides, there's no dialogue, so it makes me look like a drunken hag!

NANASE. But I really think that this piece will inspire a revolution in the world of comedy.

AZUSA. Listen, dumpy, who needs a revolution? Are you trying to make fun of me or what?

NANASE. No, that's not what I'm …

AZUSA. *(pointing at **HIDENORI**)* And, do you really think you can make that miserable looking fellow laugh?

*(**HIDENORI**, naked from the waist down, is bent over double, with his pants around his ankles. He is overtaken by a coughing fit.)*

NANASE. *(to **HIDENORI**)* Are you all right? *(to **AZUSA**)* It's all my fault. I gave him the cold.

AZUSA. Why are his pants down?

NANASE. That's how he takes his temperature.

*(The thermometer beeps. **HIDENORI** slowly removes it from his rear end.)*

HIDENORI. It's 102.

AZUSA. Are you kidding? You better go see a doctor, man.

HIDENORI. *(to himself)* If I laugh, I'll get better, won't I?

*(**HIDENORI** puts on a flu mask.)*

AZUSA. Impossible! You haven't laughed in six years! First of all, that's weird. And then, you've asked her to make you laugh, a girl with absolutely zero sense of humor!

NANASE. Azusa! Okay, let's try a short comedy skit. I wrote the script.

AZUSA. You?

NANASE. This time, it'll be full-on dumb slapstick. Here you go. It's called "At the Minimart."

(**NANASE** *hands the notebook to* **AZUSA.**)

AZUSA. *(looking at the notebook)* Are you sure this is gonna work?

NANASE. Yes, I'm sure! We have to make it work for Daddy's sake! Ready? *(announcing)* "At the Minimart!"

AZUSA. *(making the sound of an automatic door opening)* "Weeeeen"

(**HIDENORI** *coughs uncontrollably.*)

AZUSA. *(entering the store)* Good afternoon, I…

(**HIDENORI** *coughs uncontrollably.*)

(**AZUSA** *repeats her actions.*)

Good afternoon, I…

(**HIDENORI** *coughs uncontrollably. He takes something out of his mouth.*)

HIDENORI. The crown…popped off…'cause I coughed!

NANASE. Oh dear!

HIDENORI. The crown…popped off…'cause I coughed!

AZUSA. What's wrong with this guy!

NANASE. I'm sorry. He's not himself…it's the fever.

AZUSA. So take him to the hospital!

(**BANJO** *enters.*)

BANJO. Hello hello! How's it going guys?

AZUSA. Banjo!

BANJO. I've been thinking about you guys, since I did introduce you. I brought you some snacks, Nanase.

NANASE. You didn't have to, but thank you.

BANJO. What's wrong with Mr. Yamane?

NANASE. He caught a cold. It's a fever.

HIDENORI. I coughed …and this crown…!

BANJO. Is he taking anything for it?

NANASE. We just ran out.

BANJO. Well then, let's go get some!

(He pulls NANASE by the arm.)

NANASE. Now? Well, all right, I guess.

AZUSA. Hey, wait a minute, Banjo… !

BANJO. *(to AZUSA)* You take care of things here, all right?

(BANJO, making sure NANASE's not watching, points at HIDENORI who's lying face down on the table, BANJO and NANASE exit. AZUSA is left alone with HIDENORI.)

AZUSA. So…"Daddy", do you have any girlfriends?

HIDENORI. …

AZUSA. If you don't, maybe I could volunteer for the job.

HIDENORI. …

AZUSA. Just kidding.

HIDENORI. …

AZUSA. Come to think of it, have you ever even gone out with a girl?

HIDENORI. …

AZUSA. Have you ever had sex?

HIDENORI. …

AZUSA. Could it possibly be that you're into her?

HIDENORI. She irritates you, doesn't she?

AZUSA. What?

HIDENORI. She always acts shy and fakes a smile, 'cause she's so concerned about the feelings of others.

AZUSA. Well, yeah, she certainly does irritate me.

HIDENORI. She's the kind of girl who makes people want to attack her. I don't like her in the least, haven't for twelve years.

AZUSA. So what happened twelve years ago? You are seeking revenge on her, right?

HIDENORI. *(looking at AZUSA)* …

AZUSA. She told me that she's waiting for it.

HIDENORI. It's not an ordinary kind of revenge.

AZUSA. I know, a revenge so awful that it's beyond human imagination, even yours, and you can't come up with it.

HIDENORI. I've been thinking about it all this time. Nothing I come up with matches the damage she's done.

AZUSA. So tell me. What exactly did she do to you?

(Lights shift from AZUSA and HIDENORI to NANASE and BANJO, walking. NANASE carries a paper bag.)

BANJO. An accident?

NANASE. My parents and Daddy's were close, and so they used to take me to his place when I was a little girl. I was an only child so I adored him as if we really were related. But then, when I was 14… Our two families were driving back from a weekend trip we'd taken to celebrate Daddy's eighteenth birthday. Daddy's dad was behind the wheel and he was a little drunk. When we came to the railway crossing, he tried to drive through even though the gate was coming down… I happened to be riding with Daddy in his family's car since they let me play my favorite music. When the car stalled between the gates, his father suddenly freaked out, and…

BANJO. He panicked?

NANASE. Yes. In the end, only Daddy and I survived the accident because we were in the back seat. But he still suffers from it, from his right knee down, he's…

(Lights shift to HIDENORI and AZUSA, conversing.)

HIDENORI. That's why I will never forgive her.

AZUSA. Right….Huh?

HIDENORI. She crushed my life to pieces.

AZUSA. Excuse me, but let me get this straight.

HIDENORI. My life has been turned upside down.

AZUSA. I understand that, but getting back to your story, what exactly did the girl do?

HIDENORI. She was riding in the car.

AZUSA. That's it? She has nothing to do with the accident?

HIDENORI. I don't remember.

AZUSA. But you're seeking revenge on her because she did something to you, right?

HIDENORI. Yes, she did it, I guess, but I don't remember it very well.

AZUSA. Wait a fucking minute! Here you are, all grown up, and you want to take revenge on her for something that you can't even remember? And it's taken you twelve long years?

HIDENORI. As long as the need for revenge remains intact, that's enough.

AZUSA. That makes no sense at all. Isn't it because of… your leg? That's it, your leg! Your plan was to be sponsored by Adidas, but because of the injury, your bright future got shattered, isn't that it?

HIDENORI. That's it. I guess.

AZUSA. I guess? Were you a really good runner?

HIDENORI. I ran track in junior high.

AZUSA. What about high school?

HIDENORI. I was in the art club.

AZUSA. In high school?

HIDENORI. I was into oil painting.

AZUSA. So, that means…

HIDENORI. But running meant much more to me than I thought! I only realized it after I was disabled!

AZUSA. But that's kind of…

HIDENORI. People realize how precious something is only after losing it! At least that's how it was in my case! That's why I will never forgive her.

(pause)

AZUSA. I don't get it.

*(Lights shift to **NANASE** and **BANJO**.)*

NANASE. After finishing high school, I went to Tokyo to temp. You know, the typical story: I wanted to start fresh in a place where no one knew my past. It wasn't working out at all, though, and I was totally lost. Then, one day, Daddy appeared, completely out of the blue. He was standing in front of the apartment. We'd occasionally been in touch with each other after the accident, but I was very surprised because it was all so sudden. Then, Daddy glared at me with those terrifying eyes and he said to me:

HIDENORI. I traced back to that point in my life when things weren't screwed up, and I came across you as the turning point.

NANASE. That's what he said.

BANJO. What did he mean by that?

NANASE. Let's say, for example, that your wallet is missing. Don't you review the actions of the day from the time you left your house? Like, I had it when I bought the train ticket. I had it when I ate lunch. Just like that, Daddy traced backward from the present to the past, step by step, until he discovered that the accident was the turning point which separated the life in order from the life screwed up.

BANJO. Even so, you guys were fine until Yamane decided on the turning point. Why did it take him six long years?

NANASE. I don't know, but I'm guessing that the grudge festered for years until finally it burst. So, as soon as he realized where it all went wrong, he hopped on a bullet train and went straight to Tokyo...

BANJO. But Nanase, you were just riding in the car together, right?

NANASE. ...

BANJO. Did you do anything?

NANASE. (pasting on a smile) I don't remember.

BANJO. And you spent six years...

NANASE. The longer it went on, the more awkward it became to ask him.

BANJO. Nanase.

NANASE. Yes?

*(**BANJO** removes **NANASE**'s glasses.)*

BANJO. Ha! Just as I suspected. They're fake.

NANASE. …

BANJO. As for your dumpy sweats, truth is they turn me on.

*(Lights shift back to **HIDENORI**'s room. **HIDENORI** rises unsteadily.)*

AZUSA. Hey, where do you think you're going?

HIDENORI. Your perfume is giving me a headache.

*(**HIDENORI** exits. **AZUSA**, alone and bored, climbs up to the upper bunk and lies down.)*

AZUSA. Whatever! You've never even had sex.

(She brushes the pillow against her body to scent it, and puts it back. Eventually, she notices the ceiling panel which has been displaced slightly.)

AZUSA. Oh?

(She slides open the panel and pushes herself into the attic up to her waist.)

Oooh?

(She pulls herself back out from the hole, and replaces the panel.)

Oooooh!

(She sits on the bed and considers her discovery.)

BANJO. We're back!

NANASE. Daddy, sorry it took us so long. Here's the medicine.

*(She finds **AZUSA** sitting on the bed.)*

Where's my daddy?

AZUSA. Dunno. He went out. Maybe for a jog?

BANJO. A jog? That'll work well for his fever.

NANASE. Jogging…

(**NANASE** *takes a quick glance at the ceiling, then meets the gaze of* **AZUSA** *who's staring at her.*)

NANASE. Is something wrong, Azusa?

AZUSA. Banjo, come here for a minute.

BANJO. What the heck do you want?

(**AZUSA** *yanks* **BANJO** *by the arm and takes him outside.*)

BANJO. *(to* **NANASE***)* Well then, I'll see you later. Get well soon!

NANASE. Thank you, and thanks for the snacks!

(**BANJO** *and* **AZUSA,** *outside the house.*)

BANJO. Hey, that hurts. What's the matter with you anyway?

AZUSA. I'm telling you, they are really strange.

BANJO. I know. I told you so.

AZUSA. You have no idea. They are much weirder than you think, Banjo!

BANJO. You mean, you got Daddy talking?

AZUSA. The guy says that he doesn't remember why he needs to take revenge, but he will anyway, because what's clear is that he has to. What the heck do you make of that?

BANJO. Nanase doesn't know why he's holding the grudge either.

AZUSA. Then why don't they just forget it!? If neither of them remembers, it's like nothing happened! Why the hell are they engaged in this revenge business if they don't remember the cause? What are they really up to?

BANJO. Interesting. Just what I was thinking. Very interesting, right?

(**AZUSA** *watches* **BANJO** *grinning.*)

What else, Azusa?

AZUSA. *(hesitating)* Nothing in particular.

BANJO. Come on. You can do better than that.

AZUSA. There is one thing I just remembered.

BANJO. What is it?

AZUSA. Back in ninth grade, the whole class had it out for her. We razzed her pretty badly. When the teacher found out, she called a class meeting. One by one, we had to stand up and explain why we'd bullied her. One kid said, "I just dislike her, that's all. It's instinct." After that, everyone said pretty much the same thing: "She makes me sick", or "She just gets on my nerves," or "No reason: that's just how it is" – right in front of her.

BANJO. Junior high kids are scary!

AZUSA. Then the teacher told us to apologize on the spot, so all forty of us apologized, bowing our heads low and saying, "We will not dislike you any more." From that day on, she was completely ignored by all of us. In order not to dislike her, we had to avoid seeing her. That was our rationale.

BANJO. I see.

AZUSA. From that day on, we completely blocked out her entire existence. That's how it was, until graduation. Yeah, that's how it was. It makes me nostalgic.

BANJO. Why are you recalling that now?

AZUSA. I'm just wondering which is worse.

BANJO. Both are terrible, if you ask me.

AZUSA. Right.

BANJO. Well, anyway, keep up the good work!

AZUSA. You want to continue!?

BANJO. Even more reason to do so, after hearing your story.

AZUSA. No, no, no! Let's just drop it! The end!

BANJO. Why? Come on. It's fun.

AZUSA. 'Cause, Banjo, I know you're trying to get close to her.

BANJO. No I'm not.

*(***BANJO*** starts walking.)*

AZUSA. I warn you, you'd better stop. It's creepy! I can't explain why, but I know that those two are really sick people!

(They exit. Lights shift to the room. Music. **HIDENORI** *is lying on the bunk bed. He brushes away* **NANASE***'s hand when she tries to put a cold towel on his forehead.)*

NANASE. I'll go make some porridge.

(She exits to the back.)

HIDENORI. Nanase - I'm going out for a jog.

NANASE. *(from offstage)* What about your fever?

HIDENORI. It's down.

NANASE. *(from offstage)* Okay, then. Have a good jog.

*(***HIDENORI*** groggily pulls himself into the attic.* **NANASE** *takes out the notebook and starts working on her jokes. She tilts her head a little toward the attic, and expresses a sense of relief, which implies that she knows she's being watched.)*

(blackout)

-10-

*(At work. **BANJO**, eating a rice ball, watches **HIDENORI** throw the switch.)*

BANJO. "Help! I don't wanna die! Stop it! I'm innocent!" Just kidding.

HIDENORI. …

BANJO. You took some time off to get healthy. Are you all better now?

HIDENORI. …

BANJO. Oops, are you upset? I was just kidding. A bad joke.

HIDENORI. I don't mind. People die when they die.

BANJO. They also survive when they survive.

HIDENORI. I've got to get going.

BANJO. Hey, wait, please. I have some questions for you. What kind of kid were you, Yamane?

HIDENORI. …

BANJO. I hate eating alone.

HIDENORI. What kind of kid?

BANJO. I mean knowing a girl like Nanase since you were small…I'm wondering if that had any effect on your personality.

HIDENORI. Kids just wail and snivel. They don't care who's cute or not.

BANJO. I see. So you're the kind who gradually becomes aware. You gradually notice that the girl you've been playing with has been getting sexier by the day.

HIDENORI. I have no idea what you're talking about.

BANJO. Yamane, you must have had terrible acne in high school. I can still see the pockmarks.

HIDENORI. …

BANJO. So I'm wondering how it felt, during that awkward age, to see the girl next door getting sexier by the day…wonder how it felt to walk together in front of others. Did you get paranoid like, "I wonder if she's ashamed of me?"

HIDENORI. I've got to get going.

    (**BANJO** *amused, watches* **HIDENORI** *exit.*)

-11-

*(***NANASE*** is massaging* ***AZUSA*** *with a portable electric massager.)*

AZUSA. Not like that! I told you, lower!

NANASE. You mean, here?

AZUSA. Why are you going all the way down? You can't do anything right!

NANASE. I'm sorry.

AZUSA. Ow...ouch!

NANASE. What's the matter? Are you all right?

AZUSA. Too strong!

*(***NANASE*** *steps away from* ***AZUSA*** *in a slight panic.)*

AZUSA. Give it here! I'll do it myself!

NANASE. I'm sorry, Azusa.

AZUSA. You really are useless.

NANASE. *(a shy giggle)* Hee hee.

AZUSA. *(to herself)* Maybe she really is an idiot.

NANASE. An idiot?

AZUSA. Hey, stop listening! Can't you see I'm talking to myself?

NANASE. Whoops, sorry.

AZUSA. What could Banjo possibly see in a girl like this? *(noticing that* ***NANASE*** *is listening)* Hey!

NANASE. Sorry! Well, I better get back to my training.

*(***NANASE*** *drops an empty tin basin on her head repeatedly.)*

What a beautiful day! *(dropping the basin)* No, that's not it. What a beautiful day! *(dropping the basin again)* Almost!

*(***AZUSA***, *using the massage machine on herself, watches* ***NANASE***.)*

AZUSA. Hey, I know you're waiting for Daddy's revenge, and that's fine, but what about the apology you owe me?

NANASE. What?

AZUSA. Like I said, I still remember what you did to me in high school.

NANASE. Yes…

AZUSA. I'm not interested in revenge and stuff like that which gains me nothing. I want you to do something that benefits me practically.

NANASE. Benefits you practically?

AZUSA. I'm just saying that you need to make up for the pain I suffered.

NANASE. How would I do that?

AZUSA. Easy. You just have to make Banjo dislike you. That's all.

NANASE. *(taking a moment to think)* Any other options?

AZUSA. *(adjusting the massage machine)* …

NANASE. You know, Azusa, the one thing I can't bear is being disliked by people.

AZUSA. So then, I'll dislike you, and believe me that's the last thing you want. I'm intense. They say I hate with so much passion that I might as well be madly in love.

NANASE. Azusa …

AZUSA. Banjo said that he wants me to meet his parents soon.

NANASE. *(taking a moment to think)*…Okay…I've got it! You want to turn the relationship around, right? You want to shake up the routine and find passionate love.

AZUSA. I guess you could put it that way.

NANASE. No problem! I can manage that. Leave it to me!

*(**NANASE** takes a cell phone out of **AZUSA**'s bag.)*

AZUSA. Hey, what are you up to?

*(Lights shift to **BANJO**, whose cell phone is ringing.)*

BANJO. What's up, Azus…Nanase? What a pleasant surprise. What? Right now? Sure. Why not? Actually, I was just thinking about stopping by. Yep, I'm in the neighborhood. I'm over by that new condo. Yep, yep. I'll bring snacks. Okay! See you soon!

*(Lights shift back to **NANASE** and **AZUSA**.)*

NANASE. *(hanging up)* He's coming, he's coming!

AZUSA. You mean, Banjo's coming here now?

NANASE. Azusa, quick! Put these on!

*(She takes off her sweats and hands them to **AZUSA**.)*

And these too.

(She hands her the glasses.)

AZUSA. Wait a sec. Why would I wear such dumpy...

NANASE. Banjo likes them!

AZUSA. What?

NANASE. They seem to turn him on, so you two should give it a shot alone first.

AZUSA. What about you?

NANASE. I'll hide in the kitchen. Try a few different things, and if it's not working, just send him to me and I'll take care of it.

AZUSA. I don't get it. What are you up to?

NANASE. Azusa, say "I love you" in a charming way.

AZUSA. What?

NANASE. Just try!

AZUSA. *(hesitantly)* I love you.

(pause)

NANASE. I know how to make romance, so don't worry. This scheme should definitely work! Let's give it a shot. We've got nothing to lose!

AZUSA. No way. It's too risky.

NANASE. Go, Azusa, go! You rock!

AZUSA. I just don't feel like this is a...

*(**NANASE** hides in the back room. Shortly thereafter, **BANJO** enters.)*

BANJO. Hello Nanase! ...Azusa? What in the world are you wearing?

AZUSA. I'm not really sure.

BANJO. Believe me, you look awful. *(He looks around the room.)* Is Nanase in the kitchen?

AZUSA. Uh-huh.

(pause)

*(**BANJO**, standing, lights a cigarette. Eventually romantic music starts playing in the kitchen.)*

BANJO. What's with the music?

AZUSA. Banjo.

BANJO. Huh?

AZUSA. Would you go to the kitchen for me?

BANJO. *(puzzled)* Uh huh.

*(**AZUSA** watches **BANJO** enter the kitchen. Shortly thereafter, the sound of a tin basin dropping, then that of a man falling down.)*

NANASE. Come here, Azusa!

*(**AZUSA** goes to the back room, then with **NANASE** carries out **BANJO** who is unconscious. They lay him on the bottom bunk.)*

NANASE. Do you want me to take off his pants?

AZUSA. I'll do it.

*(**AZUSA** mounts **BANJO** and puts her hands on his belt to undo it, but stops in the middle and ponders.)*

NANASE. Azusa?

AZUSA. Sorry, but this isn't quite what I had in mind.

NANASE. It isn't?

AZUSA. I know you went to a lot of trouble to knock him out, but...

NANASE. What part don't you like about it?

AZUSA. I guess the rape part.

NANASE. But if he gets you pregnant, we'll be all set. We'll take a photo and offer it as proof, and that way Banjo won't be able to leave you.

AZUSA. *(humoring* **NANASE**, *as if she were a child)* That's true. But what I really and truly want is to… go to Disneyland and share cotton candy. We'll take pictures together in a photo booth and choose the heart shaped frame. So I'm not really into a plan that'll mess things up later.

NANASE. Is that right? I should have asked you beforehand about your likes and dislikes. Judging from your appearance, I thought you wouldn't mind.

AZUSA. No, I'm not at all like that. I'm no good at rape, even though it may look like I should be.

NANASE. I had no idea. So, what should we do with Banjo now?

AZUSA. …

*(**NANASE** and **AZUSA** look down at **BANJO** who is unconscious.)*

AZUSA. Did he see your face?

NANASE. I attacked him from behind so, no.

*(**AZUSA** grabs her bag and clothes and rushes to the front door.)*

NANASE. Azusa, where are you going?

AZUSA.. I'm going home, so you take care of the rest.

NANASE. What?

AZUSA. Whatever happens – even at the cost of your life, make sure he doesn't find out I was involved. From the start, I haven't been here, got it? You have to take full responsibility.

*(**AZUSA** exits.)*

NANASE. Oh no! What should I do?

*(Suddenly, **BANJO** grabs **NANASE** by the wrist.)*

BANJO. Nanase… *(He tries to get up.)* Man, that hurt. What's going on?

NANASE. Um…um…

*(Lights shift to the outside where **HIDENORI**, who is coming home, and **AZUSA**, still wearing sweats, run into each other.)*

HIDENORI. I want to ask you a favor. Please don't visit us anymore.

AZUSA. You think I'm visiting by choice? No way! My day job's hard enough.

HIDENORI. Then why?

AZUSA. It's because you guys are up to weird shit, and Banjo's hooked on that. If you want him to leave you alone, try to be normal. Stop doing crazy stuff and live a normal life like a normal person!

HIDENORI. I am normal.

AZUSA. Oh really? You don't remember the cause of the accident, you can't come up with a way to avenge your grudge, you throw the death switch without a blink, and you haven't laughed once in six years, and still you call yourself normal?

HIDENORI. …

AZUSA. Oh, and we shouldn't forget that you enjoy spying from the attic.

HIDENORI. *(looking at* AZUSA *in surprise)* …

AZUSA. How long have you been doing that? Are you aware that in the eyes of society you are a complete freak?

HIDENORI. What's wrong with keeping a close eye on the object of revenge? When I watch like that, I'm always thinking.

AZUSA. Why don't you admit that you want to have sex with her even though you don't like her? You do want to have sex with that girl, right? But after all this time, you're in no position to ask for it, so you sneak peeks to get your kicks.

HIDENORI. You're one to talk.

AZUSA. Why not ask? She'll let you do it right away. I tell you, she was very active in high school. *(pause)* All the boys at our school said that she'd never say "no." It's true. That girl would sleep with anyone. She didn't say no when her friend's boyfriend asked her. What do you think of that? She's totally hopeless.

(**HIDENORI** *walks toward his house avoiding* **AZUSA**. **AZUSA** *yells after him.*)

AZUSA. She knows that you're peeking and she's still at it!

(*Ignoring* **AZUSA**, **HIDENORI** *tries to open the door, but, hearing voices inside, he freezes.*)

BANJO. I see. My memory's a bit shaky cause of the head bump, but was that you, Nanase, looking like Azusa?

NANASE. Yes, something like that.

BANJO. Wow. I can't recall a thing. Sorry for the trouble.

NANASE. The trouble?

BANJO. Of lugging me to the bed – you did it all by yourself, right?

NANASE. Um, yes, but it wasn't too bad.

(**HIDENORI** *steps away from the door and exits to the back of the house.*)

BANJO. What am I doing? I'm here thanks to your special invitation, Nanase…

NANASE. My invitation?

BANJO. Everything's all right now, so we can get to the point.

NANASE. The point?

BANJO. Well, I've been aware of it for a while. Actually it's pretty obvious. It's hard not to notice the ambience.

NANASE. …Oh that!

(**NANASE** *hurries to the kitchen to turn off the music, then returns.*)

That was um…

BANJO. Sweats look okay on you, but this outfit suits you much better.

(**NANASE**, *realizing that she's in her underclothes, hurriedly wraps herself in a small towel.*)

NANASE. No, Azusa has my clothes, I mean, no, she wasn't here, so…

BANJO. I gather that you're seducing me.

(**BANJO** *draws close to* **NANASE**. **HIDENORI** *appears in the attic – he knows another way to get up there from the outside. He peeks down through the panel.* **BANJO** *takes* **NANASE***'s face in his hands, and closes in.*)

NANASE. *(on the verge of crying)* Um, um, um…

BANJO. Huh? *(pulling away a little from* **NANASE***)* Did I misunderstand something?

NANASE. Ye…Yes… *(She nods several times, smiling.)*

BANJO. So, it was all my misunderstanding? Well, it did seem a little strange, being that it was so sudden.

NANASE. I…I'm sorry that I didn't explain myself well…

BANJO. Still, it's not a big deal, is it?

NANASE. …?

BANJO. Well, because, Nanase, like you said before, when you lead someone on, you're prepared to take responsibility.

(**BANJO** *takes* **NANASE***'s wrist and pulls her closer.*)

NANASE. Um, um, um…

BANJO. We can't stop now, can we?

(**BANJO** *mounts* **NANASE**.)

HIDENORI. …!

(**HIDENORI**, *feeling deeply uncomfortable, crawls to the panel where he usually climbs in. He silently opens the panel, and starts to speak.*)

HIDENORI. St-St… /

NANASE. *(raising her voice to drown out* **HIDENORI***)* If I do it…

(**HIDENORI** *freezes.*)

NANASE. If I do it, will you treat Azusa well!?

BANJO. Azusa?

NANASE. That way, neither of you will dislike me!

(pause)

BANJO. I see. Got it…No problem. Will do.

(**BANJO** *removes the towel which was covering* **NANASE***'s body.* **HIDENORI**, *feeling powerless, drops his head and starts crawling toward the other exit…*)

(*…but slowly crawls back to the hole and starts peeking down.*)

(*Music*)

(*Blackout*)

-12-

(A few days later. **HIDENORI** *and* **NANASE***'s room.*
HIDENORI *reads in bed while the other three play a
board game.* **AZUSA** *is sitting next to* **BANJO***, leaning
on him.)*

AZUSA. Oh my god! Look, Banjo, I got six again! What
should I do? I'm on a roll. I love this game. I just love
it, Banjo.

BANJO. Good for you.

AZUSA. I'm thirsty. *(She drinks juice.)* Wow, this juice is good!
It's sooo good, Banjo!

BANJO. Good for you.

AZUSA. Here, you drink some too!

(BANJO *and* **AZUSA** *drink together from the same glass
using two straws.)*

NANASE. Daddy, do you want me to spin for you?

HIDENORI. You don't have to ask every time.

NANASE. Here we go!

(She spins the roulette wheel.)

AZUSA. *(looking at the wheel)* Look at that! The wheel spins
so well.

NANASE. Three. *(She moves* **HIDENORI***'s piece.)* Daddy, this is
your chance for stardom. Want it?

HIDENORI. *(giving the matter serious consideration)* Yes.

NANASE. All right. You've given up your job at the trading
company and joined a chart-topping boy band. For
your music lessons, you need to pay one million yen
in advance.

HIDENORI. That much?

AZUSA. Your turn, Banjo. Spin, spin!

BANJO. Right.

AZUSA. Two, it's a two. Number two!

BANJO. I heard you the first time.

NANASE. Let's see… You're getting married.

BANJO. Even though I'm unemployed?

NANASE. You'll have a baby.

BANJO. I can't afford tuition.

NANASE. You're due a one hundred thousand yen gift from each player for your bridal and baby showers.

AZUSA. *(paying the money)* But in real life, you have a secure job in the public sector.

BANJO. You could say that.

AZUSA. Banjo, remember how the senior director has been harassing me at work?

BANJO. Yeah.

AZUSA. If you think it's a good idea, I'm willing to quit my job.

BANJO. I don't mind.

AZUSA. You mean, you don't mind me quitting my job?

BANJO. I mean that I don't mind you keeping it.

NANASE. *(to herself)* Oh no! We've been snatched up by a corporate raider.

AZUSA. But why?

BANJO. Think about it. You're already 26. I don't want to see my girl getting bossed around by the teenaged manager of a burger joint.

AZUSA. But …! I just don't want any guys, other than you, touching me anymore, and…look! *(taking a resume out from her handbag)* I've already updated my resume, and am interviewing for a part time job!

NANASE. Daddy, your agent is asking if you want to write a tell-all exposé of your band and get major media attention. Will you write one?

HIDENORI. *(after serious consideration)* I'll write one.

NANASE. An ex-member of the band has sued you for libel. The case will be brought before the Supreme Court.

HIDENORI. The Supreme Court!?

BANJO. What kind of job are you applying for?

AZUSA. Spokesgirl at the auto show.

BANJO. Huh. *(looking at her resume)* The stuff you wrote here won't fly for that.

AZUSA. You don't think so?

BANJO. Certainly not. Spokesgirl is a competitive job. Okay, I'll rewrite it so you'll get hired.

AZUSA. That'd be great!

BANJO. First of all, why did you say that your hobby is reading?

AZUSA. It's a lie, but…won't it work?

BANJO. They'll think you're a bookworm. Let's change it and say that your hobby is "buck naked!"

(He writes it in.)

AZUSA. Huh? What does it mean that my hobby is "buck naked?"

BANJO. It means that you take it all off once you're home, and get naked. They're not gonna make you show it, so it's a good idea to blow their minds.

AZUSA. I see. Got it.

BANJO. For your future goals, why don't we put "kill the President," so that they know you think big. For your assets put "slutty" and for your flaws, let's put "Most of my relatives are ugly." Okay?

AZUSA. Are you sure that I'll get hired with this kind of…

BANJO. Don't you trust your boyfriend?

AZUSA. Of course! I trust you! 'Cause you're my boyfriend! Thank you! I love you to death, Banjo!

*(She throws herself at **BANJO**, embracing him.)*

BANJO. I love you too.

AZUSA. I love you to death!

*(She throws herself at **BANJO** again.)*

BANJO. I love you too.

AZUSA. I love you to death!

(She throws herself at **BANJO** *again.)*

*(***BANJO***, who was laughing, gets angry and slaps* **AZUSA** *on the cheek.)*

AZUSA. …

BANJO. You better get going or you'll be late.

AZUSA. Yes.

*(***AZUSA*** *grabs her bag and exits.)*

NANASE. The game.

BANJO. What?

NANASE. It's your turn, Banjo.

BANJO. Right! Sorry I got distracted. Let's stop playing. We only started because that girl made a fuss about it.

NANASE. Well, I don't mind, but…

(She looks at **HIDENORI**. **HIDENORI** *closes his book and climbs down from the upper bunk. He walks toward the door.)*

BANJO. Yamane, are you going somewhere?

HIDENORI. Jogging-time.

BANJO. So would you get us some rice balls or something?

HIDENORI. What kind?

BANJO. Any kind is fine.

HIDENORI. I'll get you a weird kind.

BANJO. I'd like a normal kind of rice ball, please.

*(***HIDENORI*** *exits.)*

BANJO. Is he faking it?

NANASE. What?

BANJO. Typical. "The injured leg actually works just fine."

NANASE. I don't think that's possible. We were taken to the hospital together, and I was right beside him when the doctor explained the injury.

BANJO. Is that so? By the way, Nanase, you cheated, huh?

NANASE. On what?

BANJO. The game. Your card read that you bought a car, got into an accident, and were hospitalized. You were supposed to receive money from each of us as a token of sympathy. You shouldn't make up stories. You need to do a better job if you're secretly going to help others win.

NANASE. I'm sorry.

BANJO. But that's your charm as well.

(**BANJO** *touches* **NANASE***'s body.*)

NANASE. …

BANJO. Is something wrong?

NANASE. Um, I don't think we should be doing this kind of … (*She starts to say something, but changes her mind.*) Nothing. Never mind.

BANJO. You do understand that if you don't let me, I'll have no reason to be kind to Azusa. And then I'll dislike you for jilting me, and tell Azusa the real reason why I was kind to her, then Azusa will hate you too… No, that's no fun. No one wins that game. For now, this is all good. Let's get past the guilt, we've done it enough.

NANASE. Yes…

BANJO. Are you all right?

NANASE. Yes…

BANJO. Well, then, that's that.

(**BANJO** *starts pulling off* **NANASE***'s sweats.* **HIDENORI** *has sneaked up to the attic and is peeking in.*)

BANJO. Do you want to do it in the bed for a change?

NANASE. But there's not much space, and… (*glancing at the ceiling*) …that could be dangerous.

BANJO. I don't mind it here if you don't.

(*Suddenly,* **AZUSA** *enters.*)

AZUSA. Hey, I came back to get my resume 'cause I forgot…

(*pause*)

…what are you doing!?

NANASE. Azusa! I want to explain…!

AZUSA. You…Is it possible that you've done it again!?

NANASE. But Azusa, it's not what you think!

AZUSA. It's not? Banjo?

BANJO. It's not, you idiot! Can't you see? This is just something that…*(thinking and talking at the same time)* … men and women do together naked.

AZUSA. Sex, you mean!

BANJO. Right. Sex…but not the kind of sex you think.

AZUSA. Sex is sex!

BANJO. Fine. Sex.

NANASE. Banjo…

(pause)

…Azusa …

AZUSA. It did occur to me…

NANASE. What?

AZUSA. It did occur to me that maybe Banjo was treating me nicely to get closer to you. I'm no fool. But I tried very hard not to think about it, telling myself, what I don't know can't hurt me, as if the thought didn't exist. If you want to deceive me, do it right! You can't do anything right!

NANASE. I'm so sorry…I only wanted to make you happy, Azusa.

AZUSA. You're the same as ever! If you're so aware of how I feel, how can you let Banjo's dick in you!? If you care about my feelings, you don't let something like that inside you!

NANASE. I…I'm sorry.

BANJO. Don't be so harsh. Nanase's crying.

AZUSA. Banjo, why are you taking her side!?

BANJO. Because you're strong. You're okay, even with this, right?

AZUSA. How could I possibly be okay?

BANJO. You're okay. You really are.

AZUSA. It's because you always play the meek victim that people think I'm bullying you!

BANJO. Hey, where are you going?

(**AZUSA** *strides toward the back room, then returns with a chopping knife.*)

BANJO. Azusa!

AZUSA. Since people think I'm bullying you, I might as well really bully you! It's all so stupid! I had to practice comedy skits every day with this irritating girl. Do you have any idea how stressful it's been for me? I've been trying very hard not to lose patience. I've been working much harder than you. You only care about not being disliked. Why don't you get it?

BANJO. Stop it! It's dangerous!

AZUSA. It's not the first time! You've made a fool of me twice!

(*She cries.*)

NANASE. Azusa, I'm really sorry.

AZUSA. "I'm only thinking of myself!"

NANASE. …?

AZUSA. Say it! "I've only been thinking of myself and nothing else!"

BANJO. What's the point of this?

NANASE. I…I've only been thinking …

BANJO. Nanase.

NANASE. I've only been thinking of myself and nothing else.

(*pause*)

How was that, Azusa? All right?

AZUSA. You really are a stupid idiot! Why don't you hurry up and die?

NANASE. What didn't you like? The way I said it? I'm only thinking of myself. Still not right? I'm only thinking of myself. It's tricky, isn't it?

AZUSA. I give up. I can't bear a girl like you. I just don't like you.

(*She tries to stab* **NANASE** *with the knife.*)

BANJO. Azusa!

HIDENORI. Stop!

(**HIDENORI** *has removed the ceiling panel and is leaning down from the attic, suspending his upper body into the room.*)

HIDENORI. Stop.

BANJO. What? Yamane?

AZUSA. (*laughing*) So, you were watching again. Who'd want to stab a worthless girl like her! (**AZUSA** *throws the knife on the floor.*) Now I get it. My apologies. If I hadn't intervened, you could have watched these two screwing to your heart's content.

BANJO. Watching…What? Nanase?

NANASE. …

BANJO. You're kidding, right? You mean, all this time we've been doing it, we've been watched?

AZUSA. I told you! These two are really sick! There's no room for you to come between them.

HIDENORI. Nanase.

(**HIDENORI** *drops down to the bed.*)

NANASE. Daddy. (*pause*) I had no idea you were doing that.

AZUSA. (*to* **NANASE**) Wait a minute.

HIDENORI. Of course, you had no idea at all.

NANASE. I had no idea, indeed.

AZUSA. What are you two talking about?

(*Music. Blackout.*)

-13-

(At home.)

NANASE. When did you start?

HIDENORI. About three years ago. I noticed that one of the ceiling panels was loose and just couldn't stop myself.

NANASE. Wait. Does this mean that you haven't been jogging? Gosh, I'm dumb. How embarrassing.

HIDENORI. It never occurred to you that you were being watched, right?

NANASE. Of course not. It's a big surprise.

HIDENORI. I bet. There's no reason to imagine such a thing.

(pause)

NANASE. Why did you do it?

HIDENORI. To consider my revenge.

NANASE. Right…well then, it couldn't be helped. But… what should we do? *(pause)* Usually, when things like this happen…living together becomes impossible, don't you think?

HIDENORI. …Maybe you're right.

NANASE. But what about your revenge? Don't you need to take revenge on me? It's all my fault, isn't it?

HIDENORI. But I forgot the cause. I don't remember a thing.

NANASE. …

HIDENORI. You don't want to live like this any longer, do you?

NANASE. Well I…

HIDENORI. Do you think we can just go on like before?

NANASE. …

HIDENORI. It's too much, right?

NANASE. Maybe it is. It's really up to you – if you're annoyed and bothered by me, then I shouldn't stay, and if you tell me to leave then I should because…

HIDENORI. All right, then. *(pause)* You can leave me.

NANASE. What?

HIDENORI. I give up my revenge.

NANASE. Are you sick of it all?

HIDENORI. …

NANASE. Of course, I understand. Any guy would get sick of spending all his time with a girl like me. I'm sorry I didn't notice earlier.

HIDENORI. But what about you? Don't you mind?

NANASE. If it's what you want, Daddy…It's what you want, so I understand…

HIDENORI. Perfect timing, huh?

NANASE. Timing? That's right, it's your birthday tomorrow. Wow! What timing. So, as long as I leave by day's end tomorrow, that'll work, right?

HIDENORI. If you want to leave so soon, it's fine with me.

NANASE. If that's better for you… *(pause)* Wow. This is all happening so fast. Well, I'm sure I can manage because I have hardly anything to take with me, but… what am I supposed to do now? I guess I should call my mom.

(**HIDENORI** *stands up and moves toward the bed.*)

NANASE. Are you going to sleep?

(**NANASE**, *as usual, gets into her own bed.*)

So then tomorrow will you….that's right, there's no more need to think up a revenge..

HIDENORI. Since this is our last night, why don't we say things that we don't really mean.

NANASE. What?

HIDENORI. We're going to say things that we don't really mean. Since it's not really what we're thinking, we won't have to read between the lines. Focus on words, and just say things that you don't really mean.

NANASE. You mean we should lie?

HIDENORI. 'Cause nothing will come of it even if we tell the truth.

NANASE. Yes. Nothing will come of it.

HIDENORI. So, it's fine to lie.

NANASE. Yes, it's fine to lie.

HIDENORI. Do you regret getting involved with a guy like me?

NANASE. …No, I don't.

HIDENORI. Do you think that you've wasted six precious years of your life living like this?

NANASE. I don't think so.

HIDENORI. Did I do something wrong?

NANASE. You didn't do anything wrong.

HIDENORI. You don't want to leave me, do you?

NANASE. I don't want to leave you.

HIDENORI. You're lying about all this, right?

NANASE. Yes, I'm lying, and this is a lie too, but if we had continued to live together, we could have been reasonably happy. I'm lying again.

HIDENORI. Even if it's a lie, don't you wish you could have been carefree, at least with me?

NANASE. Then you wouldn't have wanted to live with me, cause I really am high maintenance.

HIDENORI. I don't like high maintenance.

NANASE. See, you don't like someone who's a handful.

HIDENORI. I'm sorry that I don't like high maintenance. I'm sorry I can't say to you, I'm all right with it even if you are a handful.

NANASE. That's okay. I've always told myself not to expect anything, so, I'm all right.

(pause)

HIDENORI. Had I known that we'd end up in this kind of situation, I'd have been more…I don't know what… There's not much left to lie about anymore, so why don't we go to sleep?

NANASE. Good night, Hidenori Yamane.

*(**NANASE** turns off the bedside lamp.)*
(blackout)

-14-

(BANJO and AZUSA wait on a street corner.)

BANJO. Nasty day, isn't it?

AZUSA. They say it's supposed to rain tonight.

BANJO. What time is it?

AZUSA. Five minutes till. But we can't get into the restaurant until half past.

BANJO. Then we've got a little time to kill. Is it close to here?

AZUSA. Yep. It's right around the corner.

BANJO. Really? I don't remember anything like that around here.

AZUSA. I think it just opened. I went there for drinks with friends and liked it a lot.

BANJO. Did you get him a present?

AZUSA. Yes. Nothing special, though. It doesn't need to be expensive, does it?

BANJO. Since we're paying for dinner too, no. *(getting bored just waiting...)* Azusa, Azusa.

AZUSA. What?

BANJO. Check out that guy over there, he looks really weird.

AZUSA. What? Where?

BANJO. Over there. See that guy?

AZUSA. Where?

BANJO. The guy in the business suit.

AZUSA. Where?

BANJO. You have to look where I'm pointing.

AZUSA. Oh, that guy. Yeah, you're right. Who's he mumbling to?

BANJO. To the billboard, I guess.

AZUSA. That's pathetic. I'm surprised to see a guy like him out here in the sticks.

BANJO. Hey, take a closer look. It's your father!

AZUSA. *(laughing)* Yeah right.

BANJO. It's true, It's your father!

AZUSA. I'm telling you to stop.

BANJO. *(sounding like an older man)* Azusa, why don't you ever come home?

AZUSA. I do visit.

BANJO. Look, here comes Yamane! Azusa, quick! Give me the stuff.

AZUSA. What stuff?

BANJO. The popper thingies! The ones we just bought at the minimart. They have little strings, and when you pull them they go pop!

AZUSA. Oh those. Give me a sec here.

BANJO. *(to* **HIDENORI***)* Oh, hi Yamane! How did you get here?

HIDENORI. By bus.

BANJO. You took a bus, did you? *(to* **AZUSA***)* Hey. What's the holdup?

AZUSA. Found them! Here you go.

(She hands a firecracker to **BANJO***.)*

BANJO. Happy Birthday, Yamane! *(He sets off the firecracker.)*

AZUSA. Happy thirtieth!

HIDENORI. Thanks.

AZUSA. Come on. You look so unhappy. Wear this hat. Let's see a little more of that birthday spirit!

(She puts a paper party hat on **HIDENORI***'s head.)*

BANJO. Hey, what are you doing? That's embarrassing.

AZUSA. I'm just trying to make things a little more festive. Look at him, he looks totally depressed. He needs a lift.

BANJO. That doesn't make it right to slap a party hat on him out here in public. You've got to think before you act. Yamane looks like a total dunce in that hat.

HIDENORI. The two of you…

BANJO. Huh?

HIDENORI. The two of you didn't break up after all.

BANJO. Yeah. Well, after all that, we talked things out, and …yep. We're still together.

AZUSA. I told Banjo everything that I'd been thinking. And then…

BANJO. I misunderstood her. Because of her manner, I thought, "Well, she's got a lot of nerve", but after listening closely, I've come to understand that she's actually quite delicate and sensitive, and I realized how much I've hurt her.

AZUSA. I revealed my true self to Banjo, and he understood me. So, I feel like I'm ready to forgive you guys for all you've done to me.

BANJO. That's silly. We're the ones who should be asking for forgiveness. Seriously, Yamane, I'm really sorry for all the trouble we caused. Of course you did peek in while I was having sex, though I think I deserved it, and certainly, it will never happen again. Mr. Yamane, please be our guest tonight. Eat and drink as much as you like! It's on us. Where's Nanase?

HIDENORI. She's not coming.

BANJO. She isn't?

AZUSA. But I made reservations for four.

BANJO. Why isn't she coming?

HIDENORI. She's leaving today.

BANJO. What?

HIDENORI. She's supposed to be gone before I get home.

(At home. **NANASE** *enters from the kitchen with her suitcase. She is dressed neatly, no longer in sweats, and not wearing glasses.)*

BANJO. Could this all be…our fault? It must be, right?

HIDENORI. We couldn't have gone on like that anyway, so this was meant to be. It's all good. Finally, I can be a normal person.

BANJO. Mr. Yamane.

HIDENORI. Where's the restaurant?

AZUSA. It's right around the corner, but…

(to **HIDENORI** *who's started walking away)*

Are you really sure that you're okay with this?

BANJO. Yamane, let's go back to your place and stop Nanase from leaving.

HIDENORI. No use at this point.

BANJO. It's still not too late.

HIDENORI. It's over. *(pause)* Let's go to the restaurant.

AZUSA. It's starting to sprinkle.

*(***HIDENORI** *walks off alone.* **AZUSA** *and* **BANJO** *hesitantly follow.)*

*(***NANASE** *is in* **HIDENORI**'s *room, making a phone call.)*

NANASE. *(in a completely different lower tone of voice)* Hello. Mom? It's me…Yes, long time no speak. I'm fine. Where's that man? Really? Nothing seems to have changed, then…No, it's not for money that I'm calling. Why are you talking to me like that? …I'm calling because…I'm thinking about coming home… to your place. What's that? Just me – I'm alone. Job? I'll look for one, but, can you please stop talking to me like that? Here I am calling for the first time in six years, and you're making me crazy. What? I'm talking normal. This is the way I talk. You're the one who sounds hostile. *(sighing)* Never mind. It's too draining. Anyway, I'm coming home. I can't talk on the phone anymore. No, I can't. I have to hang up. Sorry, I'm hanging up.

*(***NANASE** *hangs up the receiver and lies down on the bed.* **BANJO,** **AZUSA** *and* **HIDENORI** *enter from where they just exited.)*

BANJO. Hey, Azusa. Which way is it? There's nothing like that around here.

AZUSA. How strange. I'd swear that it was nearby the last time I came.

BANJO. You're sure that the minimart is on the way, right, so which way from here? Straight ahead, or back the other way?

AZUSA. Ahead!

BANJO. You said back a minute ago, remember?

AZUSA. Then it's back.

BANJO. What do you mean by "then"? You don't remember, do you?

AZUSA. Ahead!

BANJO. Straight ahead?

AZUSA. Back!

BANJO. Which is it? Don't get us lost. Yamane, I'm so sorry. I'll have her find the way. *(to* **AZUSA***)* Come on!

AZUSA. But I…

(She notices **HIDENORI** *starting to chuckle.)*

Hey, what are you…

BANJO. Mr. Yamane?

HIDENORI. *(laughing)* I remembered. I just remembered.

BANJO. About what?

HIDENORI. I remember! I remember!

AZUSA. The reason for revenge?

HIDENORI. I remember it! I remember it now!

*(***HIDENORI***, laughing his head off, throws away the umbrella and runs off.)*

BANJO. Yamane! Wait! Let's take my car if you want to go home!

(pause)

AZUSA. I don't know what's going on, but I think we'd better follow him.

BANJO. Let's go!

*(***BANJO*** *runs off.)*

AZUSA. I said "follow", not "run"! Wait for me, Banjo!

(NANASE rises from the bed. She removes the calendar from the wall, crumples it, and throws it in the waste basket. For a short while, she simply stands in the room. Then, when she is about to leave with her suitcase, HIDENORI, out of breath, enters with BANJO who's giving him a shoulder to lean on.)

BANJO. Yamane, you can't run at all. You'd have much more stamina if you'd really been jogging all this time.

NANASE. Daddy…

HIDENORI. Don't leave, Nanase.

(He walks toward NANASE unsteadily, and knocks over NANASE's suitcase.)

I remember…the cause of the accident. I remember it clearly! You are to be blamed. We cannot wipe it away!

NANASE. What?

HIDENORI. You said "back up!" That's why! When our car got trapped between the rail gates, I told Dad to go forward. But you said "back up", so Dad got confused and panicked…It's all your fault. If only you hadn't said anything!

NANASE. It's my fault…?

HIDENORI. That's right! It's completely your fault! I have to take revenge on you! I certainly do!

BANJO. I'm so glad that you remembered, Yamane!

(He's getting excited for HIDENORI.)

HIDENORI. I am going to take the worst revenge on you!

BANJO. That's right! The worst revenge! Although he hasn't come up with it yet!

(HIDENORI and BANJO are laughing their heads off.)

Look, Yamane's laughing his head off! Azusa, take a picture!

(AZUSA starts taking pictures of HIDENORI.)

AZUSA. *(with hesitation)* Excuse me, but may I…?

BANJO. Hey, don't ruin it!

AZUSA. But I just realized…

BANJO. What now?

AZUSA. After all, these two survived because they were sitting in the back seat.

BANJO. Yeah?

AZUSA. So that means that backing up was the right thing to do. Wasn't it?

(pause)

BANJO. What are you talking about?

AZUSA. I mean, if the car had moved forward, all of them could have been killed, right?

BANJO. *(thinking for a moment)* Was that the case, Mr. Yamane?

HIDENORI. …

(He is frozen on the spot with a blank look.)

NANASE. Daddy…Mr. Yamane …?

HIDENORI. It's all my fault?

NANASE. No, that can't be.

HIDENORI. You weren't the cause?

NANASE. No, that's not true.

HIDENORI. It's all MY fault?

NANASE. It's me. If I hadn't said something confusing, we all would have survived the accident…!

HIDENORI. That's a lie. It was too late, wasn't it?

NANASE. No, no, no, no, no! We would have made it in time!

HIDENORI. …

NANASE. This is the truth! I'm not saying it because I'm worried about your feelings…Think about it! Why would I want to keep this grudge going by lying to you? I was nearly free to go back to a normal life. No sweats, no glasses! Why would I want to lie and have you hate me again? It makes no sense. No sense at all if I may say.

HIDENORI. …

NANASE. It's true! True true true true true! Why don't you believe me! I'm telling you the truth! Why don't you…!

HIDENORI. That's enough. I understand.

NANASE. No, you don't. You think I'm defending you.

HIDENORI. I don't.

NANASE. Yes, you do! It's quite clear to me! I'm always imagining what people are thinking. It's quite clear to me! Be so kind as to stop! Be so kind as to stop second guessing my words! Please do tell me the truth! Please do tell me what you are really thinking!

HIDENORI. Stop it, Nanase.

NANASE. I don't care anymore! There's no hope anyway! I don't care what you think of me…!

HIDENORI. Nanase.

NANASE. You yourself have said that if you can't see it with your own eyes, then you don't consider it real. So you can decide that the accident wasn't my fault, and that you won't watch me from the ceiling anymore, and that, from your perspective, I no longer exist, and never even have. And then you'll go on with your normal life. After all this, you can just walk away and get on with your life. My heartiest congratulations! Seems like you'll have no problems! I went to a lot a trouble to have you watch me, but now it's all come to nothing….!

HIDENORI. You mean the ceiling, you did that?

NANASE. Like I said before, I am a handful – the sort who plays cheap tricks, the sort who provokes a disagreement right before walking out the door. This is who I am: a handful of a woman…! Yes, I see. You are sorry that you ever came to make such a discovery. You didn't want to spoil your memory of the relationship. How sad! I am so sorry to disappoint you. Now that I have utterly disappointed you, let me say one more thing straight from my heart. What I wanted you to say is that it's okay to be a handful! I wanted you, Mr. Yamane, to accept me as a whole, trouble and all! Fucking hell!

(**NANASE** *kicks over the table. After catching her breath…*)

NANASE. This is it. The end. And now, best that I disappear.

(*She starts to exit carrying her suitcase.*)

HIDENORI. I got it.

AZUSA. What?

HIDENORI. I finally figured out my revenge.

BANJO. What are you talking about? Have you been day-dreaming? This is not the time to…

HIDENORI. (*to* **NANASE**) I figured out how to make you suffer the most. You'll blame yourself for the rest of your life. You'll see…

(**HIDENORI** *wanders unsteadily toward the door, opens it and disappears into the darkness. After a short pause,* **BANJO** *yells after* **HIDENORI.**)

BANJO. Hey, where are you going, Yamane! It's pouring outside. Hey, wait. Take an umbrella!

(*watching* **HIDENORI** *exit*)

He's gone.

AZUSA. Did you see how weird his eyes were?

BANJO. What do you mean weird?

AZUSA. …

BANJO. What are you talking about? Yamane's eyes have always looked weird.

AZUSA. No, they haven't.

BANJO. Fine, they haven't, for Chrissakes…I better go look. I'm not sure why, but I really am worried.

AZUSA. Banjo, take an umbrella!

(**BANJO** *and* **AZUSA** *exit quickly.* **NANASE** *stands alone in the room, dazed. Eventually, voices are heard from outside along with the sound of rain.*)

BANJO. *(from offstage)* Yamane!

(Fearing the worst, **NANASE** *is heading toward the door when* **AZUSA**, *carrying an umbrella, comes running back at full speed.)*

AZUSA. He ran out! Right into traffic! Unbelievable! He flew straight up into the air and /

NANASE. *(interrupting)* That can't be. People don't fly /

AZUSA. *(overlapping)* They do too! I had no idea!

BANJO. *(from offstage)* Azusa!

AZUSA. Ambulance! No…police? Whichever! Call them! Hey, what's so funny? We're in deep shit! I mean, what if he's already dead!?

BANJO. Azusaaaa!

AZUSA. Oh man!

*(***AZUSA*** *runs offstage.* **NANASE** *is alone. The lights dim as the dark waltz from the opening plays.)*

-15-

(A few days have passed. The room is empty. **HIDENORI** *enters awkwardly. Both of his arms are in casts, and his body is wrapped in bandages.)*

HIDENORI. I'm back.

(No one responds. **HIDENORI** *sits on the lower bunk of the bed.)*

It's hard to kill a human being. It was pretty much just my fingers that got severed. It'll be hard to continue with my current job, though…There's one thing that's become clear from all this.

NANASE. *(from the kitchen)* What's that?

HIDENORI. *(looking at his fingerless hands)* All I ever wanted to do was paint.

*(***NANASE*** *enters slowly from the back room. She's wearing the sweats and the glasses. She is holding a plate.)*

HIDENORI. It's all your fault.

NANASE. Want some apples?

HIDENORI. No, I don't.

(The two smile conspiratorially. Music rises.)

(blackout)

-The End-

Lightning Source UK Ltd.
Milton Keynes UK
UKHW020956131220
375066UK00009B/263